A Portrait's Lifelines

A Portrait's Lifelines

by

Yolanda R. McCulloch

DORRANCE PUBLISHING CO., INC.
PITTSBURGH, PENNSYLVANIA 15222

All Rights Reserved
Copyright © 1998 by Yolanda R. McCulloch
No part of this book may be reproduced or transmitted
in any form or by any means, electronic or mechanical,
including photocopying, recording, or by any information
storage or retrieval system without permission in writing
from the publisher.

ISBN # 0-8059-4305-6
Printed in the United States of America

First Printing

For information or to order additional books, please write:
Dorrance Publishing Co., Inc.
643 Smithfield Street
Pittsburgh, Pennsylvania 15222
U.S.A.

A Portrait's Lifelines

Chapter One: Stefonia 1

Chapter Two: Beginning the Portrait 6

Chapter Three: Early Teen Years 9

Chapter Four: Mid Teens to Young Adult Lifeline 11

Chapter Five: Ending Twelve Years of Public Schools 14

Chapter Six: Growing Up 17

Chapter Seven: 1960 through 1974 23

Chapter Eight: 1975 through 1994 26

Chapter Nine: Spring 1995 30

1
Stefonia

Binoculars? Why would anyone be looking at Stefonia through binoculars?

It was an early spring morning when Stefonia decided it was a perfect time to take a walk in one of her favorite places. She had completed drawing an illustration to be used in one of the short stories that she had written. The artwork was lying on the studio floor among other drawings and paintings. Also, copies of other short stories that Stefonia had written were stacked on the bookshelves in her studio's reference section. Visible, was another illustration to receive the necessary copyrights for another story Stefonia wrote. Daily, Stefonia would check her mailbox located inside the local post office to see if the copyright was there for her to pick up.

The studio was on the second floor of Stefonia's residence. It was the home built from Stefonia's unique design, and was suitable for her husband's and her needs.

Stefonia felt fortunate to have this convenience. The studio had both northern and eastern daylight exposure, exactly as designed in Stefonia's sketches.

After having had an early breakfast, Stefonia walked up the flight of steps from the first floor and up to the second floor studio. The warm spring morning appeared extremely bright with the sun shining through the studio windows.

Stefonia sat at her worktable ready to begin another art project. Suddenly, she had an urge to be outdoors in the sunny warm weather.

Leaving the studio and going down the stairway, she gave some thought of taking a walk in one of her favorite nearby places. She didn't stop to change her dress attire. The dark green jeans and long sleeved country shirt were appropriate for the warm sunlit morning. To get to her destination, Stefonia would drive her car the short distance from her home. With this goal in her mind, within seconds she was in the garage walking toward her car.

The car was equipped with a wooden carrying case. In it was a portable easel, a few tubes of paint, colored art pencils, and other materials used for artwork. It had a small section that kept note pads ready for Stefonia to use should she want to write quick notes. Often, the written notes were used by Stefonia at a later time while she wrote other short stories. A diary she had been writing was in the case, also. It was among the note pads.

As Stefonia backed the car out of the garage, she noticed the wooden case was lying on the back seat of the car. Usually, she kept it in the car's trunk. She remembered that the last time she used it, rain caught her by surprise. The weather had gone from sun to rain. It was easier for her to put the carrying case on the back seat of the car rather than get wet from the rain while putting it in the trunk of her car.

With the car out of the garage and having closed the garage door, Stefonia was back in the driver's seat and on her way to the absolutely gorgeous water rapids surrounded by Pennsylvania's mountainous terrain and some of nature's wondrous beautiful sights. It was in the Laurel Mountains.

Anxious to get to her destination, Stefonia did not make the stop at the post office as she drove on past it. She arrived at her destination and drove into the parking lot. She parked the car facing the rapids. It was a spectacular view!

It was a scenic display as the sun gleamed brightly on the flowing water. The water was glowing and it appeared to have diamonds sparkling throughout its rapid movement.

As Stefonia got out of her car, she paused to take in deep breaths of the fresh morning air. Then, she walked closer to the rapids to see more of the spectacular scenery. Having taken in a few moments of the natural beauty, Stefonia began to walk following a path surrounding the parking lot area. Having walked the pathway several times, she then walked toward a three-tiered platform that was made of wood. It was designed for public usage that allowed safe viewing of the rapids at a much closer range.

At each level of the platforms, one could stand and enjoy the beauty of the rapids. The platforms were different heights above ground. The lowest platform was approximately twenty–two steps lower than the tallest level of the three tiers. The lower level offered the closest view of the rapids rushing over rocks making a powerful and forceful sound of strength. It was there that Stefonia stopped to get a closer look at the natural wonder.

The amount of time Stefonia spent standing on the platform didn't matter. She felt peaceful and relaxed observing the movement, sound and sight of the water flowing so freely and so forcefully. She reminisced about some of the other natural surroundings she had observed throughout her lifetime, including a few islands.

Mid-morning was approaching as other people with an interest in the rapids made their appearance. Stefonia left the platform and was making her way back to her parked car. Instead of returning to the car, she stopped to sit on a bench that was located near the rapid's edge. Sitting in the sun and having it shine on her face made it feel so warm and even more relaxing. She felt as though her face was tanning and she was sure that she would have had a sun tan on her body if she had been wearing other clothing in place of her jeans and country shirt.

While peacefully sitting on the bench, a thought interrupted. She had previously considered painting a portrait of herself. Being relaxed and in the mood to paint, equipped with a sketch pad in the car, her thought began to develop.

Stefonia left the bench, went to her car and removed the supplies she needed from the carrying case. She returned to the bench that was situated on level ground. There was enough smooth area to put the portable easel in place. Stefonia was ready to begin the painting of a self portrait.

It was amusing to her that she would choose such a place for portrait painting rather than to sketch a drawing of the area filled with the beauty that one could only imagine, if not there. Anyone that had known or knew Stefonia would not be surprised at the decision she made. Stefonia did have an air of freedom that made it acceptable for her to do as she pleased. She didn't always follow the strict rigid rules that had been taught to her. She didn't follow rules when she painted either.

There were times that critics referred to her painting style as open and showing signs of naiveté. Some of her work was nonsubjective. This reflected a small part of Stefonia's free spirited personality.

The abstract paintings that Stefonia created as nonsubjective were usually bold in appearance. It was the use of color that motivated Stefonia to paint nonsubjectively.

When it came to understanding people and their actions, Stefonia felt that people did what was best for themselves. If one's life style, or one's taste was proper and correct for one person, it didn't necessarily mean that it was proper and correct for someone else. Her philosophy was, "Different strokes for different folks." Everyone was entitled to make their own choices. Other thoughts crept into her mind, or, as she would say, her "think tank." The thoughts were occurring in a rapid pace.

Returning to the self portrait she planned to sketch, Stefonia felt that being over middle aged, there would be many different lifelines to paint and deal with. She would paint the portrait adding or deducting facial age lines and signs that would appear. She would work it out as she dealt with her image.

The portrait painting was about to begin. A minor problem surfaced. There wasn't enough space to place the mirror she would use for self imaging. Eventually, the mirror was strategically placed on the easel in a position that allowed Stefonia to see her image.

Another challenge faced her. Sunlight was reflecting brightly onto the mirror. Stefonia thought of how elated she would be if she could capture the brightness of the glaring light in any painting, subjective or nonsubjective. How magnificent it would be!

The reflecting sunlight coming off the mirror caused another interruption. It brought tears to Stefonia's eyes. Along with the teary eyes there was blurred vision. Blurred vision wasn't the thing to have while trying to paint. Perhaps it wasn't a good idea to attempt the portrait painting at this time. It would not work as well as Stefonia would have wanted. She would paint at home where she spent time writing and doing artwork and working with other hobbies.

Having changed her mind and dealing with blurred vision, Stefonia rubbed her eyes in an attempt to stop the tear flow. Blinking as she tried to focus, she looked across the rapids. Surprisingly, she thought she saw a male figure looking in her direction through binoculars. Stefonia blamed the blurred vision as seeing someone that probably was not there.

Stefonia picked up the paraphernalia around her and began walking back toward the car. Her curiosity began to get the best of her. Was it possible that someone was watching her through binoculars?

As she walked away, she looked back to face the direction she thought she saw the male figure. This time she was sure she was seeing someone on the other side of the rapids. The person waved to her. Reluctantly, Stefonia waved back using her right arm and hand. Her left arm and hand had the load of carrying the art supplies.

In the parking lot, Stefonia reached to the car's back seat taking out the carrying case that had been left there. Carefully, most of the art supplies were put back into place. She left the sketch pad out of the case. In addition, she removed the diary that was in it. Stefonia placed the sketch pad and the diary on the front, passenger side seat of the car. The wooden carrying case was going to be placed in the trunk of the car where it belonged. Stefonia opened the trunk and placed the case next to a picnic basket that had become a part of the extras that traveled with her. The wicker handmade picnic basket had its contents, too.

With the trunk neatly packed, Stefonia was once again in the driver's seat of the car ready to move on. The clock on the car's dashboard indicated that it was a few minutes after noontime.

Stefonia had the car's ignition key in her hand, but she didn't immediately start the car. She wasn't going anywhere. Instead, she began to daydream as she sat behind the steering wheel. She didn't have any intention of leaving in any hurry. She was perfectly content. As she was taking in more of the scenery in front of the parked car, it appeared to her that the rapids were sparkling more brightly than before. She was at peace and reclined the seat. With the window of the car slightly down, she thought she would sit at the site, in complete comfort, for a short time listening to all the sounds the rapids forceful flowing water made.

As the early afternoon sun was warmly reflecting inside the car through the windows, more tears flowed down Stefonia's face. The sun was extremely bright.

Beginning the Portrait

Sitting in the car completely relaxed and enjoying the spring weather, Stefonia looked over to the sketch pad and the diary lying on the seat next to her. Mentally, she began to sketch the portrait of herself. She would relive what she termed her very own personal lifelines, the ones she earned. She began from her beginning.

After her birth on June 23, 1935, Stefonia's early childhood years were spent in a town that had a prime industry producing fine china and china used in hotels. The town also had steel mills and other businesses. The location of Stefonia's birth town was in the western part of Pennsylvania, between Erie and Pittsburgh.

An Amish area surrounded the northern part of the city that had rolling hills and farmland. From the Amish culture, Stefonia learned at an early age that not all people used an automobile or truck for transportation purposes. The Amish used horses and carriages.

Stefonia didn't live far from an amusement park that had once been known for it's natural beauty and cascading waters which flowed through rock formations. It had plenty of natural landscaping surrounding it. It had amusement rides and other entertainment, including a large dance pavilion that attracted bands with musicians providing the big band sound. The Fourth of July fireworks were displayed in a spectacular and attractive manner. The display attracted large crowds. The exhibition was always grand. The park's image slowly diminished and no longer attracted the large crowds that it once did.

The Second World War was taking place and, in most families, if not all, the concern and daily subject for conversation was the war. Although young in years, Stefonia was mature in sensitivity, especially toward friends and relatives that had family members fighting in the war. The military people were fighting overseas in foreign places for

A PORTRAIT'S LIFELINES

a just cause. It was more than Stefonia could comprehend. She witnessed much sadness during those years. She remembered the rationing of many items and how the supplies were distributed among families. There were stamps given to family members allowing their limits of sugar and other grocery store items. Stefonia didn't know where the rationing stamps came from, or who provided them. She remembered talk about a shortage of things and the stamps were the fair way of sharing the shortages.

In elementary school, air raids would take place. Stefonia had been taught certain procedures to follow if an air raid siren went off. There were practice drills interrupting classes. Each student was to keep quiet and follow the instructions given by the teacher.

Obeying rules was no problem for Stefonia. At home, she was taught to respect rules. Respect was important to her parents, relatives, neighbors and friends.

Remembering the war years, Stefonia would consider painting the portrait showing sadness in her eyes, or, maybe not. It was just a thought.

She went on to recall that after school activities included going to a branch of the town's public library. There Stefonia would choose books to read and take them home. She always enjoyed reading as a hobby. She also enjoyed gymnastics, dancing, singing, and collecting dolls. She was never bored.

Visiting the zoo in Pittsburgh and the long ride to get there was another of the happy times Stefonia spent with her parents. Other fun times with the family included the picnics at nearby lakes. The largest of the lakes where picnicking took place was Lake Erie. Those trips would begin early on a Sunday morning in order to arrive at a decent time. Without today's super highways, usually the drive back was in bumper to bumper traffic.

As for dancing, watching a Betty Grable movie in the local theater is how Stefonia learned to dance the Charleston. (Stefonia moved her feet, under her seat, following Betty Grable's movements). Stefonia, immediately went home after that movie to demonstrate her talent, dancing the Charleston. She felt so grown up teaching her friends and their teen–aged sisters how to do the Charleston steps.

Stefonia's doll collection was an interesting one. Her favorite doll had eyes that would open and close. It had a nylon type of hair, a medium brown color. It wasn't until she began approaching her teens that the collection wasn't as important to her as it had be͞e͞

The Second World War was over and peace made relaxed. Her friendship with a certain school classma was still important. Destiny went to church, played jacks, and did numerous other things along with Stefonia. Destiny was Stefonia's best friend.

Becoming a teenager meant that being a member of the school rhythm band would come to an end. Stefonia and Destiny were members of the band that consisted of tambourines, moroccos, sand blocks, triangles, and other instruments that jingled and jangled.

On a regular basis, the band performed for parents, neighbors, school faculty and others. The musical group dressed in white and wore red capes as their dress code.

They also wore hats made of illustration board. Each year the hat style was different. It was designed and shaped by the art teacher. One year the hat was shaped as a triangle, red and white in color with a string tie made to fit under the chin. Another year, the hat was round in shape, three inches in height, and had red dots glued onto it.

It was with pride that the band played their musical instruments following the music teacher's conducting signals. Stefonia's favorite instrument was the drums. The boom sound it made was loud and clear. She felt important when she played the drum. Her second favorite instrument was the tambourine.

Rhythm band was a fond memory from elementary school. She would remember her art teacher and all of the other teachers. Stefonia had respect for them.

Stefonia was growing taller and continued to keep a lanky body figure. Noticing makeup and getting enough courage to shave hair off her legs was the making of another facial lifeline. Stefonia was entering the teen years.

Early Teen Years

The way Stefonia dressed and how clothes looked on her became important to her. Buying ready made clothes in proper sizes to fit the way Stefonia wanted wasn't easy. An alteration or two wasn't the solution. The problem was resolved with her mother's help. Stefonia learned to sew.

Patterns for sewing were being altered and restyled. Having had an interest in sewing as a teen, Stefonia's mother encouraged her to further develop her sewing skills. Her mother thought Stefonia could enhance her skills by becoming a clothes designer. To that advice, Stefonia would reply, "We'll see."

Also, her hair with it's natural curl and wave became one of Stefonia's priorities. The longer Stefonia let her hair grow, the more distinct the waves became. Peers would give her compliments and make flattering comments about her sandy to medium brown colored hair.

During middle school years, Stefonia and Destiny attended the Friday night football games. Cheering for the high school team and being a part of the crowd demonstrated their support for the team. The atmosphere created by the cheering crowd gave morale support to the coach and the team members representing the high school football group.

An extra curriculum for Stefonia was to sing in the mixed chorus. Occasionally, Stefonia had a solo part to sing in the school plays. The singing talent lasted a couple of years until Stefonia lost interest. Stefonia gave up singing, even though the music teacher had hoped that she would not.

As the teen girls, including Stefonia and Destiny, experimented with makeup, some of the teen boys demonstrated their maturity. Before morning classes, in an alley behind a row of garages across from the school's front entrance, a group of teens would light cigarettes and smoke them. By hiding behind the garages in the alley, the school faculty would not see their grown-up act. After the cigarette butts were stamped out, the teen boys made their way across the street and into classrooms.

Stefonia's parents probably weren't aware of the hide and seek activity. The rules were, "No Smoking."

Television sets were becoming household items. They provided entertainment in one's home. In place of listening to the radio, Stefonia began watching a television screen. There were comedians, bands, talent search programs, movies, and much more offered as home entertainment. Commercials became a part of the television scene and advertising via television became popular. Some of the commercials had catchy tunes as part of their ads.

Another sign of a more modern way of living was the use of fewer and fewer clotheslines. Automatic clothes washers and dryers were becoming household items. And, to add to the wonder of automation, a machine was invented to wash dishes. The electrical appliances were becoming more sophisticated. The electric typewriter was making typing easier.

The dedication that Stefonia and Destiny had for each other grew stronger. They were spending more time in conversations about boys and their future goals and ambitions. They confided in each other, teen to teen, and gave their moral support to one another when needed. These were more signs of growing. It was another lifeline to consider in painting the portrait.

4
Mid Teens to Young Adult Lifeline

At age sixteen, Stefonia had her driver's license. Her parents had put limits on the time Stefonia was allowed to drive the family car. There were restrictions on the distance she was allowed to drive, and on where, when, and why she drove. Stefonia respected her parents wishes knowing well that if she didn't, the result would be no driving.

Stefonia and her friend began working a part-time job. Stefonia was able to spend her income as she chose. She learned quickly that budgeting wasn't as easy as she thought it would be. She liked math related subjects but the spending didn't always add up to her desires or expectations.

On the weekends that Stefonia and Destiny had as free time, they would spend it together talking "girl talk." Attitudes, behavior, and personalities of their peers would enter into their conversations.

One of the more serious discussions took place at the old mill site. They drove to the old mill that was a few miles east of the city's limits. The mill was located at the edge of a stream surrounded by large-sized rocks. The rocks were tall, big, and wide and stood high above the water flowing between them. Some rocks were large enough that more than one person could sit on them if their tops were flat. The beautiful natural setting at McConnell's Mill included a covered bridge.

Stefonia and Destiny used their jumping skills to jump from one rock to another. The key was not to slip on the rock's surface or fall into the stream. Cautiously, the rock jumping would take place.

As Stefonia and Destiny were sitting on their claimed rock, Destiny began telling Stefonia how hurt her feelings were. The conversation was about Destiny's sister and the young man she dated.

Destiny confided and trusted Stefonia with the reason she felt hurt. Destiny explained that her sister had a side to her that confused her. It devastated her when her sister antagonized her in front of the boyfriend, and together they would gang up on her and call her names. Destiny would be put in a position to defend herself and then matters got worse and not better.

Stefonia was sensitive to her friend's frustration. She was trying to understand the behavior of negative name calling. Name calling never made any sense to her, even when she had seen it applied to others. Stefonia became concerned with her friend as she witnessed the hurt on Destiny's face.

One purpose Stefonia could think of as to why anyone would lower themselves to name calling was that it was out of jealousy. Stefonia kept the thought to herself. What other purpose did name calling have? It was powerful mouth usage over Destiny's informative growing years.

For Stefonia to express that malice was the intention of Destiny's sister bullying would only hurt Destiny more. Ganging up on Destiny and deliberately wanting to hurt her made less sense. Why were the sister and boyfriend playing the name-calling game?

While sitting on the rock, crushed by what her friend was saying, Stefonia gave a sigh of relief. This was the first time she felt good about being an only child. She used to feel that she was short changed by not having any sisters or brothers. On the other hand, perhaps her sisters or brothers would treat her with respect.

Stefonia tried to give an explanation as to what might have been going on with the immature behavior of Destiny's sister and boyfriend. Stefonia did have thoughts in her mind that she thought would be best to suppress. She was concerned that the negative name calling could have an impact on Destiny's self esteem. She suggested that Destiny avoid being in her sister's company when the boyfriend was with her. If Destiny was out of their sight, she wouldn't be in any position to have to defend herself. To this advice Destiny asked, "Why does anyone have to hide from anyone in their own home?" Stefonia did not have an answer to the question.

Destiny did manage to smile when Stefonia made a comment that perhaps the boyfriend had a warped sense of humor. She thought to herself, or maybe he is just obnoxious. Perhaps he was sarcastic.

The subject did change when they began discussing a dance affair that they had planned to attend. It was to take place the following week. The outfits they were going to wear became the priority.

A PORTRAIT'S LIFELINES

Taking note of the time, they realized that if they left the old mill area, they could make it into town and have time to shop. They left the old mill site and drove to town.

The trip into town was a success. They bought something new to wear to the dance. Stefonia bought a pair of shoes, and Destiny bought herself a dress.

Before leaving the shopping area, they stopped at a snack bar inside a corner restaurant. While waiting to buy themselves an ice cream cone, Stefonia turned her head to look toward the snack bar's seating area. Stefonia recognized twin brothers who were in a booth sitting, They were frequently at the local public library where Stefonia worked.

The twins were happy to see Stefonia and invited her over to their booth. They expressed appreciation and satisfaction with the help Stefonia had given them. The guidance she gave them from the reference department got each of the twins a good grade on their reports. While chatting, the twins properly introduced themselves, since Stefonia didn't know them by name. In turn, Stefonia introduced them to Destiny.

A rapport began among the twins, Stefonia, and Destiny. As they talked about the dance, the twins asked Stefonia and Destiny if they would join them in attending it. The invitation was accepted and further arrangements were made.

The double date went well and much fun and laughter was shared. As time went on, the foursome spent much time together dating and going places

When the twins spoke of their high expectations in the future, Stefonia gave them moral support. She knew the importance of being there for a friend and being understanding. Stefonia encouraged their goals and expressed confidence in them. The twins had polished manners, and kept positive attitudes concerning their future. She was sure they would succeed.

5
Ending Twelve Years of Public Schools

As she entered the high school's front entry, Stefonia thought about how quickly the summer months had gone by. She was a senior and had other responsibilities to contend with. This was the last year that she and Destiny would have together as classmates. They had separate goals for themselves. Their friendship was strong, but different personality traits were surfacing. Each was unique in their own way. More signs of becoming an adult were showing. Stefonia continued having a sense of humor and was more outgoing than Destiny. It didn't take much to get Stefonia to join in on an impish act.

They both wrote letters to the servicemen that had left their homes to fight in the Korean Conflict. Stefonia wondered if the world's people would ever learn to get along. Then she remembered how some people in her surroundings behaved. It wasn't always pleasant to be around them.

Stefonia still had in her possession lines that were written in a book that her grandmother had given her. The first quote her grandmother wrote on the cover page was, "Speak softly but carry a big stick."

The first quote was followed by a lengthy set of lines.

> If a child lives with criticism,
>   the child learns to condemn.
> If a child lives with hostility,
>   the child learns to fight.
> If a child lives with ridicule,
>   the child learns to be shy.
> If a child lives with jealousy,
>   the child learns to feel guilty.

If a child lives with tolerance,
   the child learns to be patient.
If a child lives with praise,
   the child learns to appreciate.
If a child lives with encouragement,
   the child learns confidence.
If a child lives in fairness,
   the child learns justice.
If a child lives with approval,
   the child learns to like theirself.
If a child lives both acceptance and friendship,
   the child learns to find love in the world."

It was becoming clearer to Stefonia that her grandmother had an insight of things yet to come for Stefonia as she witnessed the world of adults.

The twins had moved on working toward their goals. They no longer were in the company of Stefonia and Destiny. The college they were now attending was much farther away than the neighboring one.

Destiny continued to have minor problems at home. She told Stefonia that she couldn't wait to leave home and live life away from her family.

Stefonia felt sorry for her and didn't have much to say, other than, "Destiny, be sure that is what you really want to do." Stefonia then expressed the difficulty she was having in both choosing a career for herself and at what college to apply to for formal training. Stefonia's philosophy wasn't working out for her in her senior year. Her comments, "Different strokes for different folks," and, "Whatever makes your boat float" didn't seem to apply any longer.

The responsibility of making a decision was one that Stefonia wanted to avoid when it came to her career choice. Her high school studies focused on the business and secretarial related fields. She excelled in her studies, but she would have preferred to be care free. Again, she knew better.

The portrait lifeline of this age could possibly show that some struggling took place in decision making. It meant several things to Stefonia. Soon she would have to put the high school years behind her. The lifestyle she once lived would be replaced with challenges. No longer would it matter that when she ate a dill pickle it had to be dill enough to make a chill run up and down her spine. The smell of fresh bread baking at home wouldn't be there either. (Coming home after school and having the smell of homemade bread baking to welcome her had been a real treat.)

Even though there was confusion of war times, life had been uncomplicated for Stefonia. Her parents still lectured respect as being necessary in one's life and they were still demonstrating over protectiveness. Stefonia wondered why her parents didn't relax a little more when it came to raising her and guiding her. Her parents meant well, and they did for Stefonia what they considered proper. Yet Stefonia wished she had more freedom. Would being an adult permit her to have the extra freedom she desired?

One of Stefonia's parent's expressions was, "What is this world coming to?" Stefonia would wonder what her parents would do if they ever witnessed a "moon shot." Wouldn't they be shocked? Stefonia hoped that she would never have to address that behavior. Her parents would have never understood why anyone would want to expose their derriere. On the other hand, neither did Stefonia.

It wasn't until the last month of being a senior that Stefonia stopped floundering in the decision of choosing a college to attend. She decided to go to the university approximately sixty miles away from her home. She would also give up her library job.

Having made the decision, Stefonia concentrated on the high school's dinner dance and other activities that would take place. This was the final chapter in Stefonia's elementary and high school years. It was the last time that she and Destiny would attend a high school function.

The dinner dance took place and the students all gave each other their best wishes. Wallet-sized pictures were exchanged among themselves and a few tears were shed as they went their separate ways. In New Castle, the graduates would be entering their future progress and development. Ne-Ca-Hi would remain an alma mater to the class of 1953.

What would this lifeline look like in the portrait? We'll see.

Growing Up

The university was located in the "big city," as termed by Stefonia and others living in her hometown. The university's "big city" had an interesting point with three rivers meeting together. The "big city" had plenty of history attached to it. It was well known for its medical centers and technological schools.

Inclines added interest to the hillsides of the city as well as the city having many other amenities. In addition, the museum, library, learning cathedral, art centers, plus much more made it a city of interest to its residents and visitors. The orchestras and performing arts held in elaborate halls could be appreciated by all and established the "big city" as a true cultural center.

The surrounding parks were a part of the city's landscape. The "big city" was a compliment to the western part of Pennsylvania.

The friendship between Stefonia and Destiny wasn't as close as it had been. They were growing apart as each continued with their individual studies working toward the goals they had set for themselves. They did keep in touch, although the time between their visits was getting longer.

The Korean Conflict was settled and servicemen were returning home. Stefonia's overseas letter writing stopped and she lost contact with some of the service people to whom she had written.

Another end came when one picked up the telephone, no longer was the voice of an operator heard asking, "Number please." The telephone operator didn't need to assist in making local phone calls. The phone user dialed a telephone on their own. How one used the telephone and the style of telephone design had changed. Automatic dialing had become a small part of communication's future changes.

During one of Stefonia's visits to her hometown, Destiny gave Stefonia unexpected news. Destiny and her steady boyfriend were engaged to be married. A date for their wedding had already been planned. Stefonia was further surprised to learn that Destiny had dropped out of nursing school. From earlier conservations with Destiny, Stefonia knew how eager her friend was to leave neighborhood, family, and friends and be on her own.

Stefonia hoped her friend wasn't making a mistake and found it difficult to be supportive of the decision Destiny had made. Considering what Destiny was accustomed to, she was marrying a man who was in many ways her opposite, with many opposites and differences. Stefonia didn't make any negative comments. Instead, she hugged her friend and wished her well. Later that night, before getting into bed, Stefonia knelt down by her bedside and prayed for Destiny.

Stefonia helped Destiny make final plans for the wedding that would always be in Destiny and her husband's memories. Any choices geared toward the memory would have to be theirs. If they were mature enough to be married, they should be mature enough to make decisions and choices their responsibility. Stefonia felt strongly about responsibility and adults making their own decisions.

It was a beautiful autumn day, all went well with the wedding. Destiny took the wedding vows and Stefonia knew that her friend would respect them. Destiny too knew about respect.

An empty feeling came over Stefonia. The feeling of emptiness could only be filled with the memories that she and Destiny had shared as children, teens and then adults. As Destiny and her husband left the wedding guests, Stefonia and Destiny hugged. Silently, Stefonia prayed that their future would be filled with happiness.

The Monday following the wedding, Stefonia was back at the university. She made plans to add additional studies to her already scheduled classes. In addition to math, science, and all required subjects, she added creative writing, live art and anatomy, interior decorating, and other extras that she considered interesting. Stefonia also felt that she was on her way to becoming a perpetual student.

What would the portrait's lifeline look like as a perpetual student? It was something to consider.

Illustrations had become a favorite type of drawing for Stefonia. She felt good about taking the live art and anatomy class. She added her own interpretation and style to the illustrations as she did to her other paintings and abstract work. An oil painting using minimal details was one of Stefonia's favorites. The upward look of the female's face, to Stefonia, represented someone who had faith, hope, and love. Also the painting had one of her favorite colors in it. The color was aqua. Stefonia would mix this color using a little blue as in the sky and a little green as used in landscapes to make aqua, which means water. Her aqua color represented air, land, and sea. The illustration had also become a favorite among students and art instructors.

It was during a summer break that Stefonia and another student she met chose to vacation together at an eastern coast island. As Stefonia and Celeste spent their mornings on the beach getting their summer tan, they would meet other vacationers sunning themselves. It was on one of the mornings at the beach that Stefonia met Trayson. Stefonia thought that he had the most beautiful eyes she had ever seen on a man.

While getting acquainted with each other, Stefonia and Trayson discovered that they had much in common. They were presently living in nearby communities. Trayson commented that he felt the world was smaller than one might think it was. The more they talked, the more they began to feel that dejavu existed. Stefonia thought to herself, *It's the eyes that seem familiar.* Their religion and religious beliefs came up as topic for discussion. Stefonia and Trayson had similar beliefs, but there was an exception. Stefonia had been raised as a Christian believing a savior had come and Trayson was taught that a savior was yet to come.

For the remainder of their vacation, Stefonia, Trayson, Celeste, and Trayson's friend spent as much of it as they could together. Trayson had already asked Stefonia if she would see him again after their return to the "big city."

After vacationing on the island, Stefonia returned to campus and Trayson returned to the firm that he and his brother owned together. Celeste began her senior year in college and was hoping she would find a teaching job immediately after receiving her degree. She wanted to teach art and she also had another goal in mind. Celeste wanted to open an art gallery. As usual, Stefonia was encouraging her and gave her as much moral support as she could possibly give.

The friendship Stefonia and Trayson shared was developing into a much deeper relationship. Within months of their meeting, Stefonia quit dating other men and Trayson quit dating other women. Their spare time was spent with each other and often they mentioned how they met on an island, even though they were only minutes away in distance back at the "big city."

The bonding they had with each other was so tight that if the world around them collapsed, neither would have noticed. When they weren't with each other, it appeared to be an eternity until they saw one another. Neither thought it was the time to demonstrate patience as they eagerly waited to be together.

Any one of the parks surrounding the "big city" became their hide–a–way. Trayson's work schedule and Stefonia's classes made it impossible for them to make time available at each others beck and call. Often, when they were together, they would answer to the time showing on a clock. They referred as having to answer to a clock rather than to their emotions. What they were really saying was that they both needed to watch the time because when they were together it went by quickly. Frequently, Trayson commented how lucky they were to be able to feel the passion they felt when they were together.

It was in the parks that their serious conversations about their goals and relationship was nourished. They would talk, embraced in each other's arms while surrounded by the park's natural beauty. They often commented about the best things in life being free to enjoy. The parks became Trayson's and Stefonia's private world. When they picnicked on the lawn of a park, it became their island. Since it was an island that they met on, other island talk became their private language. Clouds, serenely going by in the sky, became their island floating away.

Small animals scurrying about were no longer chipmunks or squirrels. They became monsters on an island. It was silly talk, but it was imaginative and creative in the minds of Stefonia and Trayson. They were, after all, in their own private world.

The many precious moments that they spent with each other possessed meaning above and beyond what anyone could ever imagine. The deep feelings they shared with each other made them feel as though they were one person. Were they experiencing dejavu? Perhaps they had known one another in another world, a previous one. The electricity they created was tremendous. To be so in love, deeply and emotionally made them feel that it had to have been spiritually.

Eventually, one or the other would have to step down from the "ultra–high in love" feeling and interrupt with, "it is time to leave" and followed by, "Note the time."

One afternoon as they were telling each other how important they were to one another, a light sprinkle began to fall. Kiddingly they made reference to the light autumn sprinkle as if their island cloud wasn't happy and it was crying tiny light tears. Or, on the other hand, the island cloud may have been happy and was crying tears of joy. The light rainfall did make it cozier for them to remain in the car and the embracing was as tight as two people in love could make it. The clock on the dashboard reminded them that Trayson had a scheduled meeting to attend out of town the following day. Time was of the essence with a plane flight and schedule to meet.

Although the drive back to Stefonia's dorm was a short one, Trayson drove with his right arm tightly wrapped around her. He held her as tightly as he could. He parked the car carefully to avoid any rain puddles that would be near the curb. He didn't want either one of them to step into one of the puddles. It stopped raining and Trayson was able to walk Stefonia to the dorm's front door without getting wet.

Trayson kissed Stefonia good-bye and as he began his walk back to his car, he kept blowing kisses to her and waving at the same time. The meeting he was attending the next morning would probably last several days or longer. Trayson would be away from Stefonia's company.

Stefonia watched Trayson drive away and stood at the dorm's entry until Trayson's car was out of sight. She was going to miss him.

The homework Stefonia had left behind was piled up next to the diary she had been keeping since elementary school, over twenty years ago. She opened the diary and began an entry expressing the love she had for Trayson. The diary was something Stefonia considered using for a final grade in creative writing. Before doing so, she would get Trayson's permission and approval since it had a few pages in it about him. She would title her diary, "An Abstract Story". Stefonia put her diary back in its place and began looking at the homework and trying to determine the priority it should be done in.

The phone rang and Stefonia answered it knowing it would be Trayson at the other end. He discussed the meeting plans and before he left he wanted to tell Stefonia once more how much he loved her and that his love for her would be forever. Stefonia expressed the same deep feelings that she had for Trayson and asked him to take care of the part of her heart that he carried with him always, no matter where he was. The conversation was a long one as it was nearing nine o'clock.

Approximately three hours later, before midnight, there was a knock on Stefonia's door. Opening the door, Stefonia was looking at Celeste. Celeste's face showed shock and disbelief. Stefonia wanted to reach out to her and support her no matter what. Instead, Celeste began talking and saying to Stefonia, "I am so sorry." She began hugging Stefonia and crying freely as she tried once again to talk, choked up by the words she had to say. "Stefonia," she began, "I wish with my whole heart that I didn't have to say this."

"What?" inquired Stefonia. The words were fading in Stefonia's ears. *No*, she thought, *it's just a bad dream.*

Trayson's father, at the funeral home, put his arms around Stefonia as she viewed the closed casket. He whispered in her ear, "Life will go on." Then he told her that unexplainable events do happen. It is a part of our lives to deal with them.

The head-on collision had taken several lives. After Trayson had landed safely from the plane trip, he had rented a car to use for transportation. As he was driving toward the hotel he would be staying in, the accident occurred. He didn't make it to the planned destination.

To sketch this lifeline in the self portrait would be painful. Stefonia spent more time than ever taking class after class in whatever subject she could. It was her way of trying to forget the misfortune of the past and concentrate on other matters.

By the late 1950s another conflict was escalating. This time it was in Vietnam. It was making the headlines and had many people concerned.

Stefonia by age twenty-five had her degree from the university for several years and had been on her own, responsible for herself. She wondered how she would portray the twenty-fifth year lifeline?

7
1960 through 1975

The big bands with musicians wearing tuxedos, starched white shirts, bow ties and trimmed short haircuts were beginning to fade. The orchestras performing for the fine arts were an exception as were some of the choirs that sang professionally. The replacements were jeans, longer hair styles, and rock stars. (The word rock had a different meaning as defined in the dictionary).

Electronic musical instruments were making the scene. Guitars were popular. Speakers to intensify sound were in demand. The waltzing and dancing where couples dipped as partners were changed to dancing styles that had partners dancing detached from one another. The swing and jitterbug dances were more toward shaking, rattling, rocking, rolling, and going to a disco. Some singing groups took bug–like names attached to a title. Louder than ever were the speakers.

Stefonia's parents expressed much displeasure at the drugs being used by young and old alike. There were many changes taking the place of tradition as the senior citizens once knew it to be.

There were students protesting the Vietnam Conflict. To keep order, military personnel got involved. Another movement taking place was the equal rights that women were demanding.

For women's wear, the mini skirt became a wardrobe item. Fabrics with labels reading "no ironing" and polyester made their debut. Men were wearing bell bottom trousers. It became stylish for men to wear colors and printed shirts in place of the all white ones.

World wide news included the assassination of President John F. Kennedy, and at a later date his brother, Robert Kennedy. Other headlines included the success of United States astronauts. Vocabulary which included outer space technology became familiar.

The computer era was making a stronger impact. Advanced electronics was promoted. Robotics was another continuous study.

Dishwashers were being installed in modern kitchens, as well as other gadgets. A garbage disposal installed into a kitchen sink was made available for usage.

Celeste during this period had married and was a teacher. She and her husband had opened the art gallery Celeste dreamed of having. Her goals were successfully accomplished.

In addition to being a guidance counselor in child development, Stefonia spoke to adult groups as an extra curriculum. Her public speaking subjects were about positive thinking, converting negative attitudes to positive ones using appropriate behavior to set examples, and learning how to grow from making a mistake.

In a classroom, students could freely discuss any problem they might be having with peers, parents, or others. It never ceased to amaze Stefonia how many times the culprit was their low self esteem. Many times, the more sensitive child was subjected to a more domineering one.

In discussion groups that Stefonia attended, many of them thought that everyone thought the same as they did. The clashes of opinions were that some of the adults actually believed there was only room for their views and no one else's. Often, when an adult became aware that they were doing this, the discussions would erupt into laughter. Stefonia again thought, "Different strokes for different folks."

By Stefonia's thirty–ninth birthday, she thought that she should have been guiding without the use of the reference books that she read out of. She discovered that she was wrong as different problems would arise. She was beginning to feel stressed out and began thinking that she might be changing jobs. Before she left any group, however, she would end her reading time with, "Respectfully yours."

Celeste was always there for Stefonia. She would listen to Stefonia when she was feeling burned out and when Stefonia was elated about someone. It gave Stefonia satisfaction when she saw someone using a scapegoat method to cover up their shortcomings change to become responsible for themselves.

In December of 1974, Stefonia pitched in as extra help for Celeste during the holiday season. She enjoyed working in the art gallery and especially enjoyed assisting customers buying art for decor or color enhancement.

It was during a cold evening that the heating elements in the gallery failed. Stefonia and Celeste recalled that their parents had coal furnaces and how they had them converted to large, bulky looking gas heated furnaces. They reminisced about other matters while waiting for a service person.

A PORTRAIT'S LIFELINES

When the service person arrived to make the necessary repairs, he was having a different problem. He wasn't sure if his car with its automatic transmission was as good as the one he had when he shifted manually. He was always able to repair the cars he drove in the forties and fifties. As Stefonia listened to the complaints the serviceman was making, she felt better about driving her car with its automatic transmission. She didn't mind driving the car with its clutch and gears to shift, but her preference was one with an automatic transmission.

As for the turn signal, she preferred using the flashing light in place of rolling down the driver's side window, putting her arm out, and signalling the appropriate left or right turn.

The heat problem was corrected in the gallery and the repairman left. Apparently, the car he was driving did get him home as Celeste watched him leave the parking lot of the gallery. Jokingly Celeste looked at Stefonia and said, "We've come a long way."

How would Stefonia's almost forty-year-old lifeline and her experiences look like in the portrait?

8

1975 Plus Twenty More Years

It was on Stefonia's fortieth birthday in June of 1975 that she began taking a deeper look into her lifestyle. She was still living in the "big city" and if she was to make a job change, or change careers, she had better do so in the near future.

She looked at what she experienced to date and how she could change things. One possibility would be for her to add more training to her present skills, or she could try something new.

How would Stefonia paint the lifeline of 1975 and the next twenty years to follow?

The order of sequence wasn't accurate as Stefonia recalled the changes she witnessed and experienced. There were many to think about.

The speedy zip code was used for postal service. A zip code following the state on an address made mail delivery easier and faster.

Advanced banking systems were being installed. One particular self serve convenience became known as a money access center. The user had a MAC card to use. It was another card to carry along with the popular charge cards.

Fast food restaurants and delivery services were making appearances in almost every city. Most of them served french fries, one of Stefonia's favorite foods.

Computers were becoming rapidly advanced. Programming a computer was not the most familiar subject for many senior adults. As the world was computerized, things were becoming fast, fast, and faster.

Body organs could be donated on a national scale of exchange.

One hospital could transfer a body organ to another. Transplants were being done by doctors that felt their patient needed one, or could benefit from one.

How one listened to music had changed too. Stefonia and her friends referred to their records as 78's or 45's (rpm) when they watched the record spin around on a phonograph's turn table. The new change was to listen to music on tapes or compact discs.

Landfills were filling up the land with discarded material; some dangerous and some not. To recycle was one way to reuse paper, glass, and other products. By recycling the recyclables, landfills would not fill up as quickly. (Another change, while Stefonia was growing up was when the garbage went to the city dump.)

Some public figures were getting reputations of being deceitful, and had other unflattering innuendos made about them. Other comments referring to character were also being made.

Stefonia's interpretation of her grandmother's quote to carry a big stick but speak softly must have been her grandmother's way of telling Stefonia to use discretion. Discretion was probably her grandmother's way of protecting herself from exploitation, manipulation, intimidation, and other negatives that can present themselves in reality. Was Stefonia's "Different strokes for different folks" in jeopardy?

When socializing and intermingling among groups, Stefonia met many interesting people. Some had jobs that sounded far more exciting and interesting than hers had been. She met and became friendly with many of the acquaintances.

Some of her new friends were homemakers. Stefonia would cringe when she heard her homemaking friends referred to as "just" housewives. These comments were another sign that times were changing. It seemed to Stefonia that the word "just" made it sound that respect for these women was lacking. Why were there such innuendos? Stefonia's mother had been an at-home mother and wife. Stefonia witnessed her mother as being a hard working person. She had been a mother, wife, had helped in family business, and had many other responsibilities. Stefonia would walk away wondering why women were put down for being homemakers.

As Stefonia had planned, she enrolled herself in classes that taught emergency medical procedures. The training lead to her becoming involved with an ambulance company. She volunteered as a professional Emergency Medical Technician, and later became a board member working in administrative duties. It was a rewarding experience to be a part of the public service. Stefonia enjoyed all of the several positions she held in the ambulance company,

Rohn, another member of the ambulance company, became a

friend to Stefonia. Much later, Stefonia learned about what the side stepping Rohn had been doing since the first time he had seen Stefonia. The first encounter that Rohn had with her became known to Stefonia as the "whirlybird" story.

Stefonia entered the crew room where Rohn was on duty. Rohn remembered her as coming in the room, walking through it to the other side, and exiting into a hallway leading to the learning center. He wondered who the whirlybird was, and made a mental note of interest.

A time came when they were properly introduced. After that, it was easy to make light conversation whenever their paths crossed. Sometimes they would come in contact with each other outside of the ambulance company. Their contacts were friendly toward each other and at times they were fun.

In one incident, Rohn was entering a parking lot filled to capacity. Stefonia and another friend were leaving the lot, as fate would have it. As Stefonia backed out the car, she managed to position her car at an angle that would not permit any car other than Rohn's car into the space. Rohn thanked her. A few days later, he called Stefonia to ask if he could take her out to dinner for being good enough to help him with the parking situation. Stefonia replied, "Sure."

The dinner invitation was accepted for a Friday evening. They had a lot of talking to do. Stefonia had mentioned that she was planning a career change. Rohn was supportive of her decision and was helpful assisting with Stefonia's chemistry class. That was one subject that Stefonia had never studied.

More changes were taking place in the "big city," and the city was saddened when their mayor died following an illness that became familiar among politicians. Other changes were taking place also.

As Stefonia had grown accustomed to having interruptions take place, her life style was once again changed. Stefonia and Rohn became Mr. and Mrs. on the day of his birthday, July 21.

They eloped and were married in the mountains that they both loved to visit. Then, property was bought in the area, and Stefonia designed their home receiving the complete stamp of approval from Rohn.

The home was not far from the famous Falling Water that was designed by the well-known architect, Frank L. Wright. Rohn and Stefonia moved into their woodland home leaving the "big city" behind. Their moving day was in spring of 1992.

During 1994, two of the women Stefonia thought well of were

layed to rest. These women, who Stefonia considered being refined and in a class of their own, were Jacklyn Kennedy Onassis and actress Audrey Hepburn. To Stefonia, they represented class, culture, and much more. They would be missed.

What would the portrait lifeline of the past twenty years look like as Stefonia was approaching 1995 and her sixty-year-old birthday was arriving?

One big change Stefonia would remember was the earring. No longer was the earring considered to be jewelry worn by women, only. Men too wore the pierced earring.

Times have changed since 1935, haven't they? Another form of speaking was called "rap" talking. Stefonia didn't think the lingo would be used by all.

In earlier years, who would have imagined using a phone in their car? The cellular phone was becoming popular. When purchasing the cellular phone, it could be bought with a portable carrying case. What other changes were in the future for communication purposes?

Automobiles had front-wheel drive, rear-wheel drive, and for transportation, the four-wheel drive was popular with some drivers. (More to think about when buying for transportation purposes.)

Spring 1995

It was after a phone call from Celeste that Stefonia learned that an art studio was trying to locate her. The studio wanted her help in the designing of a large canvas drop cloth to be used as a background for a stage play.

The design, if possible, was to have an illustration similar to the one Stefonia had sketched years ago. It was the illustration showing the facial interpretation of faith, hope, and love.

Arrangements were made for Stefonia and Rohn to stay in the "big city" while Stefonia worked on the section of the canvas she would be responsible for painting. The canvas would have its mural designed and painted by several other artists living in the area. Other stage props for the play would be made after the canvas mural was completed.

Rohn was involved in decisions on how to construct certain props. His mechanical engineering knowledge was useful and appreciated. Most of his ideas and plans were being put into use.

About a week went by when Stefonia's illustration was near completion. A few small touches were left to paint and Stefonia would have the illustration completed to her satisfaction.

An interruption occurred. The sound of sirens and much confusion began taking place around her. For awhile, Stefonia wondered if she had returned to Emergency Medical Technician duties. If so, why didn't she know?

The following day, trying to focus on her surroundings, Stefonia was being awakened by a voice asking, "Stefonia, why are you weeping?" That question was followed by other questions.

What was happening? What was going on? And why such strange surroundings? Questions were coming into her mind more and more as she desperately tried to open her eyes and focus.

A PORTRAIT'S LIFELINES

She could hear encouraging words, but she didn't understand why. As she was able to focus more clearly on the people surrounding her, she was amazed at what she was seeing.

The male voice leaning over the bed and asking questions was the same man looking at her through binoculars. The man across the water rapids of Ohiopyle. She focused on several paintings that had been scattered around the room. One particular illustration was the faith, hope, and love one. It was displayed on a portable easel with a male figure sitting in a chair next to it. He wasn't asking questions.

Instead of Stefonia answering the man leaning over her asking why she was weeping, Stefonia turned toward the blue-eyed man that was sitting next to the easel. He was wearing a gold earring in his left ear, heart side of his body. She asked him, "Why are you weeping?" His answer, "Mine are tears of joy, dear."

Becoming more alert, Stefonia recognized that she was in bed in a hospital room. There were bandages on her face that felt hot to her touch.

The sirens she had heard was that of an ambulance transporting her to a hospital in the "big city," Pittsburgh. (The hospital wasn't far from the university Stefonia had attended).

The surgery to her face required her to be sedated. Stefonia remembered that it was a nurse standing next to her in the operating room saying, "Stefonia, think of a place or places that you find relaxing, comfortable, and peaceful." That Stefonia did! First she put herself in her studio at home then she went to Ohiopyle's water rapids. The green jeans and country shirt that she was wearing in her dream was really the hospital gown.

The man watching her through the binoculars was the doctor looking at her facial injuries through magnifiers used for surgical reconstruction. The reluctant wave to the man looking at her through the binoculars occurred when the doctor had been trying to determine how much damage was done to her left arm.

The bright sun shining on her face was the bright light of the operating room. Then there were more hanging bright lights placed low, near her face.

The sewing skills that she learned as a teen were actually the sutures. (A big difference in sewing machine stitches and surgical ones) . As the stitches were being put in place on Stefonia's face, it must have been when she had been dreaming of how fast things were changing. The doctor performing the surgery had to close the wounds quickly.

The reminiscing was Rohn reading to Stefonia out of her written diary, "An Abstract Story." He was reading to her because of the uncertainty of Stefonia's memory. She could have had a problem remembering the accident or worse, she could have amnesia. The impact signs across her forehead turned out to be of minor concern to the doctors examining her. The damage was limited to her face.

The illustration was placed in the hospital room to help stimulate Stefonia's mind, if need be. The self portrait Stefonia had been painting in her dream came from the combination of Stefonia being sedated and Rohn reading parts of her diary out loud for her to hear.

Stefonia's right hand wasn't holding art supplies, as in her dream. It was Rohn holding her hand for support. Rohn, while holding her hand was praying; showing his faith, his hope, and his love. Stefonia had in her life some of the important ingredients for happiness. It gave her the desire to survive the accident, and she knew Rohn was there for her.

The journey Stefonia experienced in her dream was her past. It gave her plenty of food for thought. She would, after the accident, keep her priorities in order. She would keep on respecting others, too.

The accident happened as she finished touching up the last segment on the canvas drawing. The final touch–up was on the braided hair of the illustration. She was pleased with the results and happy that the project was near its end. It was up to other artists to complete the oversized canvas mural. Stefonia wasn't paying attention to the position she was in while standing on the ladder to take another look at her work. Down she went, face first.

Fortunately, the braid was on the lower part of the drawing, or Stefonia could have been much higher on the ladder. Keeping her positive attitude, Stefonia thought, *It wasn't as bad as it could have been.*

After a few days in the hospital, Stefonia was ready to be released. Her soon–to–be sixty year old reconstructed face was still under bandages. She would be making trips back and forth between the mountain home and Pittsburgh. Rohn would be with her to help her through the ordeal.

Before returning to their home in the woodlands, a part of the Laurel Mountains, Stefonia would make an in–between stop. The stop would come after leaving Pittsburgh and after driving to the top of the scenic Summit Mountain. Along the way home, Stefonia and Rohn's priority would be to stop at a mountain shrine and count their blessings. Stefonia would include a prayer with the words, "will be done on earth; as it is in Heaven."

A PORTRAIT'S LIFELINES

In less than five years, many will witness the ending of the twentieth century. Another century will begin. What will make history?

Will people turn to faith and hope and learn to love one another? Will people learn respect?

Notation

Stefonia (the fictitious character) and I have similarities. They include having the same birthday and being familiar with the mentioned natural settings in Pennsylvania.

In the story, the diary referred to as "An Abstract Story" has the same title that my personal diary has. The contents are different. One day, my diary "An Abstract Story" may be written for publication.

As for the changes in the story that are now history, I can only ask, "Remember?"

The story is fiction.

Respectfully yours,
Yolanda R. McCulloch